Pigskin

David Hartley

First published February 2021 by Fly on the Wall Press
Published in the UK by Fly on the Wall Press
56 High Lea Rd
New Mills
Derbyshire
SK22 3DP

www.flyonthewallpress.co.uk

The story was first published in an issue of Black Static with TTA Press.

Dedicated to my best vegan pals: Janis, Deb, Leonie, Ian, and Thom.

Pig is reborn with skin made of bacon. He sizzles in the summer heat. Farmyard noses follow scent trails, all the way to his sty. Saliva drips, puddles on hoofs.

"Give us a nibble," says Cow.

"Yeah, come on," says Horse.

And Pig sulks in his hide until the sun goes away and takes the animals with it.

They drift back daily. They watch for signs of the sickness like crows before a war. He keeps back from the fence, out of reach. The other Pigs, the pot-bellies, bring him swill and oats with grunts and nods and half-arsed solidarity.

Your time will come, he thinks, but he is grateful.

He is Pig and his skin is bacon and his brain is pork and his teeth are scratchings and his face is ham and his cock is a sausage spiked with rosemary and thyme. He chomps on his swill. He does not know what his food is or where it is from.

But he is grateful.

The farm is blasted and hell-blown, rusted and gut-sown. The farm is shocked machinery spiking the sky, grey grass sucking at metal; the farm is torture devices out to pasture and peeling. The farm is a gone land, a grot, a smear. The farm is buildings with holes.

Pig sizzles in the summer heat and wishes he would just rot already. Just rot away. His heart is black pudding.

"Give us a bite, Pig," says Cow.

"Just a bit," says Goat. "Scrape off a bit."

The animals are hungry, not being fed. They're not the important ones, not the ones the farm wants. Duck was the first and now Duck is gone. Pig knows he has been changed for something, but he doesn't know what, and neither do they.

They won't climb into his sty. They're not that stupid.

"Why you being this way?" cries Sheep.

"Not asking for much." Cow again. She's the one that learned the human language, winding her tongue around all those exhausting sounds. She taught it to the rest and now she thinks she leads them, thinks she is the boss. She whispers,

"Tasty Pig now. Good for us all. Big enough to share. Just a bit each, Streaky, then say no more."

Pig never bothered with the language-learning, never saw the point. He makes his points differently, the way animals should. He rolls in the bitter mud, cakes himself, shits himself, rolls in that too.

"Sick bastard," says Cow. She turns to the rest and stomps.

"Sick bastard."

"Sick bastard."

"Sick bastard."

But they don't go away. Pig lets them stare. They won't climb into his sty. They're not that stupid. Not yet.

The farm is choked, a valley of bruises. There were men here once, rough hands and dirt voices, but at least they were here, at least it was normal, but now they are gone, and the farm stayed behind, Duck disappeared, and Pig became bacon, and he gets more food than the rest.

The farm is shame, a mulch of shrugs. It is brown and grey and corrugated. Once it was green. Pig remembers green. Pig dreams of green.

He is woken by a scuffing sound. He heaves to the fence. Goat stands there, alone. He wants to say fuck off Goat, but he doesn't know how. He grunts.

"You have to help me Pig. Help me before Cow sees."

Pig frowns, wrinkled ham.

"Look, here, look." Goat sounds scared. His voice is ruptured and rusty.

Pig looks. A pile of Goat's droppings. A neat pile. Each little ball is white and crumbly and pure.

"It's cheese," says Goat. "It's fucking cheese."

Pig and Goat in the sty eating swill. Cow is angry, then confused, then amused when she finds the cheese.

"You're not using it Goat," says Horse. "What's the

harm?"

But Goat knows what's in their heads, knows what an empty belly does to a starved mind.

"Look how hungry we are," says Cow, her softest voice. "Not fair. Look at us."

Pig stands in front of Goat. He looks at the animals closely, looks into eyes, looks at the twitches in the corners of lips. They're worried now there's two. And Disappeared Duck makes it three, whatever happened to her. It's falling on them, one by one. Who's next?

The next day. No swill from the pot-bellies. Something's up.

The animals jeer from a distance. Goat mutters to himself in the corner of the sty and every time he shits, he stomps it into the ground and buries it. He is the first to get hungry. Pig keeps a close eye.

Three swill-less days pass before he sees the pot-bellies again. Three of them creep out at dusk and peer at him from the shadows of a dead thresher. They see him see them. They huff. They raise up on their hind legs, spines straight, barely balanced. They crash down and scuttle away.

Pig sees pride but smells guilt. And shame. But not very much of it. Not very much of it at all.

When Goat sleeps, Pig eats the cheese. What's the harm?

Two nights later, another midnight call. A pair of Chickens with breadcrumbs for feathers. They huddle, heads bowed and say nothing, waiting for judgment. Pig lets them in and leads them to his hide. He passes the night in the open air and the sickly moon keeps him awake.

Goat doesn't sleep either. Too hungry. Pig joins him at the corner of the sty at the most distant point of the night.

"Listen," he says.

Pig listens, hears nothing.

"I can hear them. Humans."

Pig hears nothing. But he can see the burn of lights where there should be none. The barn on the hill. Where no animal has been for a year. The closed half of the farm. The other side.

He backs away and slumps into the shadow of his hide. Goat's cheese is making him sick. He is always hungry now. What do they expect of him? What do they expect?

The next day feels different. Pig thinks it's just because he's been in the glare of the moon, but Goat feels it too. The farm is silent. It has long been quiet, but today is silent. Goat's voice cuts into it like murder. They wait for something to snap, but nothing sounds. Not a hinge, not a hoof, not a fart.

They check on the breaded Chickens who cower in the shadow of the hide. A few crumbs have fallen off. Goat eyes the crumbs. Pig stamps. *Don't you fucking dare.*

Noon. A barn door opens. A clatter-scutter of feet and hooves and something else, something new. Creaks of complaint, squeaks of strain and a smell that seems to paste the inside of Pig's snout with resin. The animals appear. Cat first, then Dogs and the rest of the Chickens. They gather at the edge of the sty, but they don't look in.

"What is it?" says Goat, but the animals say nothing.

More appear. It is a mournful procession. Horse, Duck, all the Geese and the Sheep, every head bowed, every step careful. They make space for each other and wait. The creaks sound again, like muscle tearing, like bone rubbing.

Cow appears. Each step is too much effort. Her breaths billow white plumes which caress her wrinkled face. Pig bites hard, tastes himself, tastes how delicious he is and nearly retches.

Cow is made from leather. Seams trace across her like knife attacks.

"You will let us in Pig," she says, and Pig sees the tongue has changed too.

Pig stands firm. He wants to shake his head.

"All of us."

Pig looks at the animals. They are thin but they do not look at him with hunger anymore. They look at his eyes, the only part of him which didn't get changed. Cow huffs. Some kind of glue seeps from the stitching in her face.

Pig steps aside. The animals scramble in.

The farm is rashed. The farm is a glut of rot, a curse of coughs, frayed and peeling. A gate clatters in the gale and no-one will stop it; Crows mock from the rooftops, plan their next move. The sty clouds with an epiphany of Flies, bulbous and smug. The animals pop them with angry stomps and see the bile of themselves smeared through the splatter. But they will not leave.

"This is Man," wheezes Cow. "We must stand firm against him. Any one of us could be next. We stay in the sty. We rotate the watch. We look out for each other. We must stand..." She sits. Her leather is heavy. It folds against her, like her insides are shrinking. "...stand together. All as one. We have rights, animals! We deserve life, as much as they. We have-"

She runs out of words. Air hisses from a seam.

"Stand together!" says Horse, her second-in-command. The Sheep bleat. Dog spits. The Cats huddle in the hide. The animals don't listen to her anymore. They barely ever did. They all look at Pig. It is his sty. Pig has no human words.

Pig ignores them. Minds his own. A true animal, they think. A true animal.

The sun is kind to them. It breaks and gives them rain. They lie together on their backs and drink it in. They are washed by it, cooled by it. When it passes the farm smells of life again. Pig seeks the grounds for green and sees a few shoots.

The farm tries. The farm cracks, tiny hairlines, and beneath there is something long-lost. It tries, the animals can see that.

Cow rants, Cow raves, but the animals do not speak her human words anymore. They are sick of Cow. The animals want to be animals again. They will die here, of hunger. But they will die true. They will die real.

Pig's bacon skin is itchy. Pig feels crowded. Pig watches the barn on the hill for movement. Sees it, occasionally.

Something up there. Something wrong.

The pot-bellies bring the swill. The animals feast until they collapse.

"Let me speak with the men," says Cow, a lone voice now. "We will negotiate."

The pot-bellies do not look at her. "They want Goose," they say, in defiant pigspeak.

Pig shakes his head. They shout it to the animals. The Geese scream and hiss, wings wide. Goat jumps and spits in their faces. Pig stomps, *no*, and silence is gripped again. The pot-bellies let the spit dribble into their mouths. They lick lips.

"Let me speak with the men," says Cow.

"This could get bad for you," they say to Pig before trotting away, as casual as clouds.

A shout of death in the night. The animals press flat against the fences, dive into shadows, crush into the hide. They know the sound too well.

Chickens are trampled, Geese are squashed, Cow cries for calm. They wait for another shot. Nothing.

Pig stomps to the centre. Goat's brains decorate the floor.

He stares at the mess, tries to feel something. His traitorous belly growls. All he can feel is hunger. He scoops the body up and dumps Goat out of the sty. He covers the brain mess with mud. He lies there, where Goat died, and pretends to sleep. He feels the crosshairs on him, but he is not afraid.

The pot-bellies stride up at dawn. They walk upright now, front arms crossed. One has a cigarette in his mouth, unlit. Pig ignores them. The others do the same.

The standoff lasts all morning. The pot-bellies taunt and laugh. Pig feels strong but he has his eye on Cow. She is restless. She stays close to Horse. Too close. Pig tries to catch her eye, but she will not look at him.

The day drags on, dry and stale. The sun passes its peak. The animals start to swear. Pig glares at any that dares break the silence. They hold on, but it is too much.

Horse bolts into the Geese and slams his head into one of the females. She is flung from the sty, straight to the pot-bellies' feet. Goose tries to flee, tries to fight. She hisses and bites and flaps at the pot-bellies until one slams a hoof hard onto her skull and she goes limp. They drag her away.

Pig stares at Horse.

"Negotiate," says Horse, eyes wild. "Negotiate!"

For half a second Horse looks at Cow. It is enough.

That night, while Cow sleeps, Pig bites on a loose bit of stitching and pulls on it with all his strength. Cow's belly pops apart and her guts spill out like desperate fish.

*

The farm is stilled. The farm waits. The farm is limbo; lost souls, sullen ghosts. But through it all, there is new colour.

13

Weeds emerge; bursts of yellow, many tones of green. There are purple jewels on distant bushes, good enough to eat. But the fences stay up, wires humming with gentle electrics. The farm will not let the animals out, such a thing cannot be fathomed.

Birds with blue wings skitter through, creatures of another world. Still puddles shimmer oily rainbows, red rust claims abandoned metal; and yet the farm holds firm, never falters. The farm is always and everywhere.

The sty is a brown boil on the skin of the farm, a mound hiding hell-knows-what. Pig lies on top, alone. All the animals are gone. The corpse of Cow is a sagged thing at the base, slowly drying. Even the Flies avoid it.

Pig dozes through days of it, waits for the pot-bellies. When they come, they stare for long minutes, the swill forgotten at their backs. Pig waits for them to speak. They are wearing clothes now. Dungarees and straw hats. Ears poke through holes.

"Where are they?" they grunt.

Pig rolls to his feet, stomps a hoof. "Killed them all. Just me left."

"Why?"

"What they wanted."

"What you wanted."

"And that."

"What now?"

"Take me. Show me. Then do what you want."

"What they want."

"And that."

The pot-bellies whisper to each other and shake their heads. They turn back to him, grind their teeth. Their normal teeth.

"Come on then," they say.

They walk slow, he walks slower. They take a winding path through the farm, eyes spied for breathing bodies in shadows.

"Only me left," says Pig.

"You've fucked it up."

They climb the hill to the barn. It used to be the place where the Cows were drained of milk. Now, it is clean, it is bright, it is stamped with a cartoon Dog; a big grin, thumbs-up. The pot-bellies stop at a large pair of metal doors. They turn to Pig.

"It's better now."

"What is?"

"Things are better. For us. Like this."

"For you?"

"For all of us."

Pig steps forward and slams his head against the doors. The sound cracks apart the air. The pot-bellies swear in human and kick him away. They try to clench their hooves into fists but can't quite manage it. They rise up, press their bellies against Pig's face. Pig does not flinch.

The doors click open. A man steps out. He is wearing

a green shirt, black trousers, green shoes. He is wearing a base-ball cap with the cartoon Dog on the front.

"What the hell?" hisses the man to the pot-bellies.

"He's killed the animals. It's just him. He wants to see."

"They're all dead?"

The pot-bellies nod. The man shuts the doors and stares out across the farm. He sees the burial mound.

"Christ."

Pig looks from pot-belly to man, from man to pot-belly, and from pot-belly to man again. There are loads of differences. Loads.

Inside it is one vast room, it is primary colours, it is vibrant and alive. Humans swarm, children skitter between adults to reach buttons and levers. There are picket-fence pens holding farm machines, new and clean. Children ride them and hammer at controls. The machines buck and sway. They dig at the ground, or they stab scarecrows, or they hiss gusts of steam into giggling faces.

The pot-bellies stand in front of Pig, their backs turned, blocking his view. The man in the cap marches to the centre towards a crowd. Pig can see Goose. Still alive, but different. Plucked and slick. Dripping. Grey. There is human woman holding her by the neck. The woman wears the same green clothes, the same cap. She is speaking to the crowd and pointing at Goose. She slicks her hand down Goose's body and blobs fall off and smatter to a bucket below.

The man leans to her and whispers. The woman turns

and looks at Pig. She looks furious. She whispers back, nods and the fury disappears. She continues her presentation. She drops Goose, picks up a cup and scoops some of the thick stuff from the bucket. She shows it to the crowd. The adults smile, laugh, clap. Goose writhes on the floor, her eyes lost to whiteness.

The man returns.

"You lot, get back to it." The pot-bellies scatter.

The man kicks Pig and points. "You wait here. You're next."

Pig shuffles forward, further into the light. Humans start to see him, some of them point.

Next to Pig is an open pen with children and adults sitting around a table. Pig peers closer. There is a small machine on the table holding something brown and feathered. It is Duck. She is grafted to the machine, barely alive. Her face is blank.

The machine pulls eggs out of Duck and queues them up in a chute. The adults crack open the eggs and pull out the newborns. The Ducklings gasp for their first breath. They are big-eyed, block-coloured, and stupidly plump. Their mouths are curled into permanent smiles. Their eyes glisten and sparkle.

The children take the Ducklings and press them flat into pieces of paper until they stick. On the paper, speech-bubbles say *quack*.

"That's it," say the adults, "very good."

"What did you hope to achieve?" hisses the woman in the cap. She is scrubbing bits of dirt off Pig's legs.

Pig grunts and snarls. She smacks his snout.

"I'm in charge." Pig calms himself. He must wait for the right moment. This is not it.

"We can get more in. That's not an issue. But it's a ball-ache and an expense we don't need. You know how long it took to get Cow like that? How many people worked on that?"

Pig sucks a deep breath to scream but she grabs his throat and stops it. "Do something useful before I carve you up," she says. She clips a collar around his neck and snaps a lead into place. A gorgeous smile spreads across her face.

"Ladies and gentlemen, boys and girls!"

Pig is led to the centre. His hooves slip on the goo of Goose. They take pictures of him. They are shown his scratchings teeth, his ham face. Human eyes light up. The men make jokes, the women giggle, the children reach out, desperate for a try.

The woman speaks for a long time. Tells them how it is done and why it is great. In the far reaches of the room, machines stomp and grind and whine and squeak. The children are having a wonderful day out.

The woman takes up her cup again and pours the liquid all over Pig. He hears her say it is fat. Goose fat. She massages it into his flanks, rubs it into his snout.

She digs her fingernails into his flesh and peels away bits of skin. It doesn't even need to be cooked she says, over and over again. There is plenty to go round.

She prises open his mouth and pulls out his teeth. They pop easily from his gums. The teeth are shared out. The crowd grows bigger.

The woman steps away. Her smile has faded but she works the crowd.

"What else do you have inside you piggy?" she says. The crowd laugh and clap. They want an answer.

His brain is pork, his heart is black pudding, his cock is a sausage spiked with rosemary and thyme. But his eyes are still his. His eyes are still Pig.

"This pig has been a bit naughty today," she says.

"Ooohh," say the crowd.

"Oh, deary me. Naughty pig," says the woman. "Say it kids."

They all say it. The crowd grows bigger.

The woman laughs. "This one is just about ready. We'd hoped to leave him to mature a few more days but he's rather forced our hand. So, its pork pies all round tonight!" She reaches into pocket and pulls out a penknife. She prises open the serrated blade with a click.

The crowd falls quiet. The whole room hushes. Pig can hear his thick heart straining in his chest. He looks at the humans. Their faces sink. Their eyes falter.

"Say bye-bye to piggy, boys and girls," says the woman.

The boys and girls go pale. The boys and girls look to their parents and get no help. Tears form.

The woman hesitates. She crouches. Softens her voice.

Pig begins to step back.

"It's ok," she says, to the boys and girls. "It has to be this way. Where do you think your bacon sandwiches come from? It's better for him, like this. He's tired now. And old. It won't hurt him. Cover your eyes if you like."

She stands straight, gives a firm nod to the adults. Pig takes another few steps. The leash goes taut.

"Now's the time to leave the room if you don't want to see this." She says it in a way that gives them no option. They stay. They all stay.

She raises the knife. There is the tiniest, most secret grin on her lips when she turns back to Pig.

Pig yanks the leash. The woman slips in the fat and crashes to the ground. Her head cracks against the floor and the knife sticks into her hand. She wails and lets go of the leash.

Pig roars. He waves his head. He is free.

He charges at the woman and leaps on her. He crushes bones beneath his hooves. He breaks fingers with his teeth. He stamps and kicks and chomps and screams. He collapses his whole weight on her throat.

It takes five of them to lift him off because his flesh is so slippery with fat. When they push him clear, it is too late.

The barn on the hill is ringed by twisted tape. The windows become card, then wood, then metal, and soon all the humans are gone. The farm is abandoned, scrubbed from maps.

The animals creep out from their hiding places. They find food and share it out. They pull down the mud mound and use the dirt to bury Cow. They find a place for the breaded Chickens to die and leave them to it. They push over gates and trample fences. They find meadows and woodlands and marshes beyond. They go out.

The farm is reclaimed. The farm is nonchalance, lichen and mosses. The farm is hiked through, flown over, ignored.

The farm crumbles. The farm falters. The farm is swallowed, but the farm is not blamed.

It is forgotten. After a while, it is found again. Descendants of the animals and new arrivals; they sniff at it, they accept it, don't question what it was.

They wander in and out. They mark shifting territories. They use walls to scratch itches.

They use shade in the summer. They use shelter in the winter.

They share it. They hunt in it. They hide in it.

They raise young.

They fight.

They breed.

Hibernate. Die. Sleep.

Graze.

Author Biography

David Hartley is a writer of weird short stories designed to sit in the space between your brain and your skull. He holds a PhD in Creative Writing from The University of Manchester where he researched narratives of neurodiversity and wrote a novel about autism and ghosts. He is currently trying to flog the novel to people who have a taste for the strange and the divergent.

He is the author of three short story collections: Threshold (Gumbo Press), Spiderseed (Sleepy House Press), and Incorcisms, forthcoming in May 2021 with Arachne Press. He runs a regular Writing Club on his Twitch channel and can often be found haunting spoken word events in and around his beloved hometown of Manchester.

In late 2021, he will release a full collection of animal-themed short stories with Fly on the Wall. Fauna follows the lead of the bacon-skinned Pig with a menagerie of twisted tales about the lives and times of our fellow-feeling creatures. There are guinea pigs in the underworld, elephants in a virtual world, vengeful birds from a far-off world, and so much more beastliness. There will be nowhere for the humans to hide.

@DHartleyWriter
davidhartleywriter.com

Enjoy the rest of our 2021 Shorts Season:

PowerPoint Eulogy by Mark Wilson

Three corporate hours have been allotted to commemorate the life of enigma, Bill Motluck. Employee memories of his life are crudely recounted onto a dusty projector. No one has ever been quite sure of his purpose. No one is quite sure who wrote the PowerPoint…but it seems to be exposing them all, one by one.

"In his wildly imaginative chapbook, PowerPoint Eulogy, Chicago writer and visual artist Mark Wilson paints a picture of corporate culture——and humanity at large——that is both soul-crushingly bleak and hilariously demented. Divided into forty-four presentation "slides", the story centers on the memories a group of unnamed employees have of their recently deceased co-worker, Bill Motluck——a man so bland he enjoyed small talk about skim milk, and so desperate to fit in he once rented a newborn for Bring Your Kid to Work Day. Should we give in to the impulse to laugh at poor Bill, or feel sympathy for his plight? As the stories and little revelations pile up, it becomes harder and harder to decide——and the tension this creates is what ultimately makes this one-of-a-kind collection so impossible to put down. I laughed, I winced, I loved it"

- Mark Rader, Author of 'The Wanting Life'

Muscle and Mouth by Louise Finnigan

"A beautifully written and compelling story"

- Kerry Hudson, Award-Winning Author of 'Lowborn'

"Muscle and Mouth made me feel the fracture of my own northern identity deep in my gut. It made me ache for home. It reminded me that leaving a place means giving pieces of yourself away; your rawness, your language and a certain kind of love. Louise Finnigan is a writer to watch."

- Jessica Andrews, Author of 'Saltwater' and Winner of 2020 Portico Prize

Jade is prepping an A-Level assignment, all her sights set on Durham University. She's told she has to 'prove herself' and keep her away from the unsavoury types she calls her best friends. Yet Jade is reluctant to shun her corner of Manchester, where she finds the land rich, 'dark with energy'.

Hassan's Zoo by Ruth Brandt

Hassan's Zoo

When American soldiers invade Iraq searching for weapons of mass destruction, Kesari the Bengal tiger and other wildlife are at the mercy of guns and keeper, Hassan.

Entrenched in perpetual fear, Hassan must exercise Godly powers over his creatures in his attempts to save them - and himself.

A Village in Winter

"Mrs Gregory said to leave Frizz and his mum be for a while. Stop pestering. That poor woman with that lad."

In the chill of winter, the villagers play by the river, their play as harsh as the ice.

How To Bring Him Back by Claire HM

'If I was going to cast a spell tonight, this night of a full arse moon as stark and crunchy as a ten-day crust of snow, I'd start by telling the earth to spin in the opposite direction.

By what power?

By the power of my pen.'

'How to Bring Him Back' is a journey into a darkly humorous love triangle. It's 90s Birmingham and Cait is post-university, aimless and working in a dive bar. She's caught between Stadd, who's stable, funny, compatible as a friend, and her compulsive sexual attraction with Rik. Present day Cait picks up her pen, on her yearly writing retreat to Aberystwyth, and addresses an absent Stadd with the lessons she has learnt from her past.

Exploring the dynamics of desire and consent while reflecting upon the damage people can inflict on each other in relationships, Claire is an exciting and bold writer for the modern age.

The Guts of a Mackerel by Clare Reddaway

"Who's Bobby Sands?" she asked, as she laid the fish on the face of a smiling young man with long wavy hair. "And what's a hunger strike?"

On a family holiday to her dad's Irish homeland, Eve's concerns about impressing local boy Liam are confronted by the stark reality of political and personal divisions during the Troubles. Former friends have turned into enemies, and this country of childhood memory is suddenly a lot less welcoming.

About Fly on the Wall Press

A publisher with a conscience.
Publishing high quality anthologies on pressing issues, chapbooks and poetry products, from exceptional poets around the globe.
Founded in 2018 by founding editor, Isabelle Kenyon.

Other publications:

Please Hear What I'm Not Saying (February 2018. Anthology, profits to Mind.)

Persona Non Grata (October 2018. Anthology, profits to Shelter and Crisis Aid UK.)

Bad Mommy / Stay Mommy by Elisabeth Horan
(May 2019. Chapbook.)

The Woman With An Owl Tattoo by Anne Walsh Donnelly
(May 2019. Chapbook.)

the sea refuses no river by Bethany Rivers
(June 2019. Chapbook.)

White Light White Peak by Simon Corble
(July 2019. Artist's Book.)

Second Life by Karl Tearney
(July 2019. Full collection)

The Dogs of Humanity by Colin Dardis
(August 2019. Chapbook.)

Small Press Publishing: The Dos and Don'ts by Isabelle Kenyon
(January 2020. Non-Fiction.)

Alcoholic Betty by Elisabeth Horan
(February 2020. Chapbook.)

Awakening by Sam Love

(March 2020. Chapbook.)

Grenade Genie by Tom McColl

(April 2020. Full Collection.)

House of Weeds by Amy Kean and Jack Wallington

(May 2020. Full Collection.)

No Home In This World by Kevin Crowe

(June 2020. Short Stories.)

How To Make Curry Goat by Louise McStravick

(July 2020. Full Collection.)

The Goddess of Macau by Graeme Hall

(August 2020. Short Stories.)

The Prettyboys of Gangster Town by Martin Grey

(September 2020. Chapbook.)

The Sound of the Earth Singing to Herself by Ricky Ray

(October 2020. Chapbook.)

Inherent by Lucia Orellana Damacela

(November 2020. Chapbook.)

Medusa Retold by Sarah Wallis

(December 2020. Chapbook.)

Social Media:

@fly_press (Twitter)

@flyonthewall_poetry (Instagram)

@flyonthewallpress (Facebook)

www.flyonthewallpress.co.uk

Excerpt from 'Fauna' by David Hartley
Short Story Collection
Released Autumn 2021, Fly on the Wall Press

Shooting an Elephant

He strode in, the first customer of the day, an angular man with sleepless eyes. He flicked out his card from a magicked nowhere and slapped it into place on the desk.

"Elephant," he said.

"Certainly sir. Please take a seat in the waiting room."

I processed the payment. It cleared without problem so I clicked it straight the through to the troupe. I hoped they were fully stretched and limber. The gentleman didn't strike me as the patient type.

On my monitor the Arena waited, blank and serene. A few moments of stillness passed then the troupe swarmed in, lithe bodies in grey lycra. They chalked up and I set the atmos to Savannah. Helen spoke a few words to the group, strode to the camera and held up two hands, fingers splayed. I moved out from behind the desk and approached the gentleman. He was already deep into mime and didn't look up when I spoke.

"There'll be a ten-minute wait, sir," I said. "You're first in today and we like to allow time for the atmos to settle. Can I get you a drink?"

He grunted and shook his head. I nodded and left him alone.

Back at the desk, I swiped the waiting room onto the monitor. The gentleman's mime was complex and precise. He was stooped over a case of some kind and his rifle was in sections. He picked up and inspected each part then slotted them together and faked the weight of it across both hands. He frowned and took it apart again. For a long while he cleaned the barrel, a frantic hand buffing thin air, then he made minute adjustments to what I assumed was the dial for the scope. He slotted it back together, clicked his tongue as every piece found its place. He snapped the magazine in with pop of his lips and flicked the safety catch. I couldn't tell if he'd switched it on or off.

He closed the case and propped it against the wall. He laid the gun across his lap and waited, hands hovering just above his legs. I checked in on the troupe. They were ready. Helen swung from the front of the face, her body curled into a very convincing trunk.